This book belongs to

....

World's Best Burper

Buddy is the Easter Bunny.
But what's hard to explain
Is if the burping
Keeps him sane.

Mama and Papa just stared
And could not explain why.
When a baby Buddy bunny
Always burped, but didn't cry.

He burps when he is eating,
It matters not what.

He burps when he's nervous,
Or put on the spot.

Buddy burps when he talks.
He burps when he hops.

He burps when he's doing
Just any old flop.

Even when he is sleeping
Buddy burps in his dreams.
He cannot control them
At least that's how it seems.

He burps around friends.
He burps when alone.
"I wish I could stop burping,"
He says with a groan.

Some think Buddy's burps
Are from a mean bunny growl.
But he burps when he's happy
Or when his mood's foul.

His burps can be smelly
When in a closed room.
They're loud and they're powerful
Like a sonic boom.

When Buddy delivers eggs
He burps into a hive.
It scares the bees,
And they flee for their lives.

Despite constant burping,
Buddy bunny still has friends.
They try to support him, saying,
"It's just one of those trends."

They say burps are rude,
And best kept to yourself.
But you can't bottle burps,
And keep them on the shelf.

Most people must burp,
And so do animals, too.
It is just something natural
That all creatures do.

It's just that Buddy bunny
Burps more than most.
If he was more vain,
I guess he would boast.

What else can you do
If you're full of gas?
I suppose you could fart,
And let wind pass.

But Buddy bunny prefers
To burp and not fart.
Some think it's crude
But, in fact, it's quite smart.

Buddy bunny is so talented.
He can burp to a tune.
His favorite song is
'Burp Me to the Moon.'

One day Buddy came home
To a girl asleep in his bed.
Buddy burped very loudly,
And Goldilocks fled.

Buddy felt a bit sad
That he scared her away.
But if you woke to him burping,
I doubt you would stay.

Buddy entered a contest
For the world's loudest burps.
Compared to his efforts,
The others were chirps.

The world's greatest burper
Buddy bunny was soon crowned.
His fame quickly spread,
He was a burper profound.

Now everywhere Buddy goes
People flock there to hear
His champion burps
To thousands of cheers.

Buddy recorded a CD
Of his burping songs.
It became a gold record
And sales are still strong.

This proves that success
Can be actually quite funny.
Just take the example of
Buddy the Burping Bunny.

You just have to find
The one thing you can do,
That nobody else
Can do better than you.

Follow us on FB and IG @humorhealsus
To vote on new title names and freebies, visit
us at humorhealsus.com for more information.

 @humorhealsus   @humorhealsus

Made in the USA
Monee, IL
29 March 2021